KING of the COURT

MW00892022

To all those who are in
need of a good friend.
—Jentry

Integrity - Ambition - Morals

Text © 2021 Jentry Youd
Illustrations © 2021 Yuliia Valchuk
All rights reserved.

No part of this book may be reproduced in any form whatsoever, whether by graphic, visual,
electronic, film, microfilm, tape recording, or any other means, without prior written permission
of the publisher, except in the case of brief passages embodied in critical reviews and articles.

The opinions and views expressed herein belong solely to the author and do not necessarily
represent the opinions or views of Cedar Fort, Inc. Permission for the use of sources, graphics,
and photos is also solely the responsibility of the author.

ISBN 13: 978-1-4621-3966-8

Published by Sweetwater Books, an imprint of Cedar Fort, Inc.
2373 W. 700 S., Springville, UT 84663
Distributed by Cedar Fort, Inc., www.cedarfort.com

Library of Congress Control Number: 2021938051
Cover design and typesetting by Shawnda T. Craig
Cover design © 2021 Cedar Fort, Inc.

Printed in the United States of America

10 9 8 7 6 5 4 3 2 1

Printed on acid-free paper

KING of the COURT

written by Jentry Youd

illustrated by Yuliia Valchuk

Sweetwater Books · An imprint of Cedar Fort, inc. · Springville, Utah

Tick. Tick. Tick.

Ty sat at his desk and stared at the clock on the wall as the loud ticking noise repeated in his head. He didn't mind school, but he would much rather be playing basketball. English, math, and science could be interesting at times, but the main reason he came to school each day was to become king of the court.

Every day at recess, many of the students would gather at the court near the playground. Some of them would choose teams and play basketball against each other. The first team to score three baskets won and stayed on the court for the next challengers. The winning team was known as "king of the court."

At Riverview Elementary, the same team always won. These three boys seemed unbeatable, and all the other teams tried their best to beat them.

Ty, Max, and Grif were always a team. Every day they would get together and create a game plan to become the new king of the court.

"Today is the day we will win," the boys would say while bumping each other's fists. Every recess, though, it never happened. Even with them playing as hard as they could, they continued to lose day after day. It was frustrating, but they kept trying and never gave up.

The undefeated team that was always king of the court had lots of basketball talent. They were quick with their dribble and could make a shot from nearly anywhere on the court. One of the boys could easily dribble between his legs and even behind his back without ever losing control of the ball. They beat the other teams by passing and using their speed. They weren't the biggest or tallest kids, but they were the fastest.

Not all the kids would play basketball during recess and lunchtime. Many kids just watched shyly and never dared play.

A boy named Andy watched closely each day from the playground near the basketball court.

Andy was different. He wasn't like anyone else his age. He was the tallest and most clumsy person in school. Sometimes he would accidentally trip over his own large feet just by walking. If he ever tried to pick up a basketball, he would struggle to dribble or shoot. His shots went so high and so far that the ball would rainbow over the top of the basketball hoop and backboard.

Andy didn't have many friends and spent most of his time alone. He was too scared to talk to anyone and became embarrassed when he got too close to where the boys were playing. He showed little emotion and kept his head down as he walked around the playground. One day a basketball bounced his way.

"Throw the ball to us, Andy!" the boys yelled. Andy didn't dare pick it up, so he softly kicked it in their direction.

As he kicked it, one boy teased, "I'm surprised clumsy Andy didn't fall over when he tried to kick the ball." All the boys laughed, and some pretended to be Andy kicking the basketball and falling to the ground.

As the days and the games went on, the same undefeated team continued to win. Ty, Max, and Grif tried their best, but they were no match for the champion team.

One day after school, the three boys got together to practice. They wanted to create a plan that would finally help them win. As they were shooting, Max said, "We just need to be taller so we can rebound the ball. Maybe a tall player could help us."

When Ty heard that, he got an idea.

"I know this sounds crazy, but what if we had Andy on our team? I know he can't shoot or dribble, but he can catch every rebound and put his hands up high for defense."

"I like that idea. It's worth a try," Grif replied. "We can all shoot great, but it's hard for us to get rebounds and play defense."

Ty then explained, "If we had him catch every rebound, he could then pass the ball to one of us to shoot. I know we'd win!"

At first they laughed at the idea, but then they all agreed to talk to Andy.

The boys were excited to get to school the next day. Before it started, they found Andy alone in the classroom, sitting at his desk, drawing pictures in a notebook.

"Hey, Andy. Do you want to play basketball with us today?" asked Ty.

Andy looked at them nervously. While slowly moving his head from side to side, he quietly responded, "I don't know how. People will laugh at me."

"We'll teach you," said Max. "We know we can win if you join our team."

After some begging from the boys, Andy nervously agreed to try. Grif said he'd sit out during the day so that Ty, Max, and Andy could play together in the three-on-three game.

The boys took Andy outside and explained to him his role on the team. They taught him to keep his hands up high to block the other team's shots and jump for all the rebounds. He didn't have to worry about shooting at all.

"Get the ball, pass the ball," Ty reminded Andy.

Recess came quickly, and as soon as the bell rang, the boys bolted outside to be the first challengers. The champion team laughed when Andy stepped onto the court.

"Good luck, clumsy," one of the boys said, looking at Andy.

Grif immediately told them to stop. "Give Andy a chance," he said.

Ty and Max gave Andy smiles of encouragement. "We got this, Andy," said Max. "Just rebound and block."

As the game began, everyone was shocked to see Andy playing. At first, laughter came from the crowd of students, but the laughing quickly stopped when one of the boys took the first shot of the game and Andy slapped the ball out of the air.

Every time the other team tried to shoot, Andy was there to block the shot or rebound the ball. Andy would get the ball and pass it to Ty or Max, just like he was coached to do. The plan worked to perfection, and the game ended in record time. Ty, Max, and Andy finally won because of Andy's defense and rebounds. The undefeated team had finally been beaten.

As Ty hit the game-winning shot, he and Max celebrated by jumping onto Andy's back. All the kids watching erupted into loud cheers.

After the game, Andy tried to hide the smile on his face by placing his hand up to his mouth and looking down at the ground. His smile stretched from ear to ear, and he couldn't hold back soft laughter. He became the hero on the court without shooting a single shot. High fives came to Andy from all of the other boys and girls who had been watching.

Ty, Max, Grif, and Andy became great friends that day. They learned the importance of being a team and working together. Being king of the court was a great feeling for the boys—a feeling they would never forget. Together they had accomplished a hard-earned goal.

To Andy, king of the court meant something different. Winning was great, but having a friend was even better. Andy was happy, simply because he finally belonged.

DISCUSSION QUESTIONS

1. Do you think Ty, Max, and Grif were good friends?
Why and how do you know?

2. How do you think Andy felt when he kicked the basketball back to the court and the other kids made fun of him?

3. What made Andy a good basketball player even though he couldn't shoot a ball or make a basket?

4. Why did Andy make Ty, Max, and Grif a better team?

5. What were Andy's strengths on the basketball court?

6. Ty, Max, and Grif became king of the court when they beat the champion team. What made Andy feel he was king of the court?

7. Which character do you most relate to? Why?

8. What is the moral of the story?

Learn more about

Integrity – Ambition – Morals

Facebook @ I Am – Character Education
Twitter @IAm_CharacterEd
character.education.i.am@gmail.com